Pretty Lady of Saratoga

TREASURED HORSES COLLECTION™

titles in Large-Print Editions:

PRETTY LADY OF SARATOGA

The story of a spirited Thoroughbred, a determined girl, and the race of a lifetime

Written by **Deborah Felder**
Illustrated by **Sandy Rabinowitz**
Cover Illustration by **Christa Keiffer**
Developed by Nancy Hall, Inc.

Gareth Stevens Publishing
MILWAUKEE

For a free color catalog describing Gareth Stevens' list of high-quality books and multimedia programs, call 1-800-542-2595 (USA) or 1-800-461-9120 (Canada). Gareth Stevens Publishing's Fax: (414) 225-0377.

Library of Congress Cataloging-in-Publication Data

Felder, Deborah G.
Pretty Lady of Saratoga / written by Deborah Felder;
illustrated by Sandy Rabinowitz; cover illustration by Christa Keiffer.
p. cm.
Originally published: Dyersville, Iowa: Ertl Co., 1997.
(Treasured horses collection)
Summary: Although her temperamental horse Pretty Lady is about to
be retired, Polly longs to see her in the winner's circle and pursues
plans to retrain her in time for the prestigious Travers Stakes.
ISBN 0-8368-2404-0 (lib. bdg.)
[1. Horsemanship—Fiction. 2. Horses—Fiction.]
I. Rabinowitz, Sandy, ill. II. Title.
III. Series: Treasured horses collection.
PZ7.F3356Pr   1999
[Fic]—dc21   99-11739

This edition first published in 1999 by
Gareth Stevens Publishing
1555 North RiverCenter Drive, Suite 201
Milwaukee, Wisconsin 53212 USA

© 1997 by Nancy Hall, Inc.
First published by The ERTL Company, Inc., Dyersville, Iowa.

Treasured Horses Collection is a registered trademark of The ERTL Company, Inc.

Printed in the United States of America

1 2 3 4 5 6 7 8 9 03 02 01 00 99

CONTENTS

CHAPTER ONE

Pretty Lady

On a sunny June morning in 1925, Polly Canfield, a pretty girl with blue eyes and golden hair, was leaning over a fence at Canfield Farm.

On the other side of the fence, in a field, horses ran, frolicked, or grazed contentedly. From time to time, the grazing horses raised their heads and touched noses with their neighbors in a friendly way.

But one horse, a filly, stood alone in the middle of the field. She didn't run or buck playfully like the others.

The horse was a three–year-old chestnut Thoroughbred named Pretty Lady. Looking at her made Polly sigh. She knew the reason the filly had lost her spirit, and it made her both angry and sad.

Just then, Polly heard the sound of a car behind her. She turned to see a snappy roadster drive up the lane and stop a few feet away from the fence. A man and a woman got out of the car.

The man was wearing a cream-colored linen suit and a straw hat with a flat brim. The woman was dressed in a white linen skirt and a long, white blouse. She wore a small, round hat that covered most of her bobbed hair, white gloves, and a long strand of pearls. She carried a blue silk parasol.

I bet they're tourists, Polly thought as the man and woman walked toward her.

Canfield Farm was located just a few miles outside Saratoga Springs, New York. Every summer hundreds of people flocked to Saratoga to watch the horse races. This early in the summer, Saratoga was just beginning to become crowded with tourists, but it would become even more so when the races began in August.

Polly wasn't surprised to see tourists at Canfield Farm. Her father, Bill Canfield, stabled and trained racehorses, and ever since she was a little girl, she had seen summer visitors strolling down the lane from time to time to watch the horses in the field.

"Hi, kiddo," the man said, grinning at Polly in a

friendly way. "We're looking for Bill Canfield. Is he here?"

"He's at the racetrack right now," Polly told the man. "I'm Polly Canfield. Maybe I can help you. Do you want to see one of the horses?"

The man nodded. "My wife and I are thinking of buying a colt named Whirlwind," he said. "I heard he's being stabled here and that Bill Canfield is training him."

"That's right," Polly said. She turned and pointed to a brown colt with a white blaze. The colt was running and bucking in a separate paddock. "That's Whirlwind over there."

The woman suddenly pointed her parasol at Pretty Lady. "Hey, take a look at that filly," she said to her husband. "She's a real beaut!"

"She's the cat's meow, all right," her husband agreed.

The couple's admiration of the filly pleased Polly. "She's the most beautiful Thoroughbred in Saratoga," Polly told them proudly. "Her name is Pretty Lady."

"Pretty Lady," the woman murmured. "I think I remember that name. Wasn't Pretty Lady the filly who showed such great form on the racetrack last summer? People said that she was a sure bet to win the Travers Stakes or the Saratoga Cup this year."

"Pretty Lady is the same filly," Polly told the woman. "But I'm not sure she's going to be racing this year."

"Why not?" the man asked.

"It's a very sad story," Polly replied. "Before Pretty Lady came here, she'd been stabled somewhere else. It was a big stable and, according to Dad, not a very good one. The owner didn't pay his hands well, and he hired whomever he could find."

"Anyway," she went on, "The groom who was in charge of Pretty Lady treated her roughly. When he rode her, she balked, and he whipped her to make her go. After awhile, she became sour and sulky. Now she won't let anyone ride her."

"Gee, that's too bad," the man said, shaking his head. "She sure is a pretty filly."

"Well, who cares about a horse that can't race, anyway," the woman said in a bored voice. She turned and stepped over to the paddock, followed by her husband and Polly. "Now, what about Whirlwind? What's the price tag on him?"

"I'm not sure," Polly told the woman in a polite but stiff tone. "You'll have to ask Dad."

"We'll do that," the man said. "Tell your father we'll be back another time, will you, kiddo?"

The man took his wife's arm, and together they

walked back to their car. Polly watched them drive away. Then she turned to look at Pretty Lady again.

"Poor Pretty Lady," she said with a sigh. "It seems like nobody cares about you anymore, just because you're not going to race."

The filly stopped grazing, looked up at a horsefly buzzing around her, and shook her head. In the sun, her silken mane flashed reddish-gold with the movement of her head.

Polly was glad that Pretty Lady had finally found a good home at Canfield Farm. She loved helping her father take care of the filly and the other horses every morning before school and in the evenings.

Now that school was out for the summer, Polly planned to spend all her time with Pretty Lady. More than anything in the world, she wanted to make friends with the nervous Thoroughbred.

From the moment Pretty Lady arrived at the farm, she had refused to let Sam, the Canfields' groom, anywhere near her. Only Bill Canfield had been able to handle her. He treated her gently and expertly, but lately he had been too busy with the other horses in his care to spend time trying to cure Pretty Lady of her skittishness.

As the weeks went by, Pretty Lady had become used to seeing Polly in the field and at her stall. She had begun to shy away less and less whenever Polly approached her. But she remained skittish, and so far, she had shied away every time Polly had tried to touch her.

Polly knew that if she could convince Pretty Lady to let her stroke her, it would be an important step in winning her trust.

Polly saw Pretty Lady head over to a nearby section of the fence, and she went over to where the horse was standing. She held out her hand to the filly. Just as she usually did, Pretty Lady snorted, tossed her head, and nervously backed away.

In the past, whenever the filly had shied away, Polly had left her alone. But as she stood watching the horse run across the field, Polly decided that today would be different. Today she was determined to gain Pretty Lady's trust.

Bad News

P olly waited until she saw Pretty Lady station herself at another section of the fence. Then, walking as slowly and quietly as she could, she circled the fence toward the filly.

As Polly moved closer, she talked to the filly in a soothing tone. At the same time, she reached into her pocket and took out a lump of sugar.

"Hello, girl," Polly murmured. "Don't be afraid. No one is going to hurt you."

Pretty Lady pricked up her ears at the sound of Polly's voice. Slowly, Polly reached over the fence and held out the lump of sugar. The filly stood very still for several moments, watching Polly.

Polly waited patiently, her hand stretched out toward Pretty Lady. Finally, with a sudden movement, the horse stepped up to the fence, lowered her delicate neck, and sniffed at the sugar. Daintily, she picked it up with her teeth.

While the filly ate, Polly reached over and touched her velvety neck. To her delight, Pretty Lady didn't shy. She stood still and let Polly stroke her. She seemed more relaxed than ever before.

"I guess I was acting nervous, and that made you nervous, too," Polly whispered to the filly as she continued to stroke her. "Everyone has the wrong idea about you, girl. I bet that all you need is some retraining, and you'll be ready to race again."

Polly remembered the first time she had seen Pretty Lady in action. Late last summer Polly had gone to a race with her father to watch one of the colts he had trained. But she could not take her eyes off the beautiful filly blazing down the track, edging past the other horses length by length. Pretty Lady had won that race with ease, and Polly was certain that with the right training she could win again.

Polly smiled as she pictured the scene in her mind. "I can just see you standing in the winner's circle with the flowered horseshoe around your beautiful neck," she said to Pretty Lady.

Suddenly, Polly's daydream was interrupted by the sound of a truck. She turned and saw her father driving the Canfields' horse truck up the lane toward the stable.

"Here comes Dad, bringing Challenger back from his workout," Polly said. "I'd better go and help him get the horse out of the truck and into his stall."

She smiled at Pretty Lady. "I'm glad we've become friends at last," she whispered. "I'll come back to visit you later, okay, girl?"

Pretty Lady nickered. Then she tossed her head proudly and trotted away from the fence. It was almost as if she were saying, "Maybe I'll let you visit me again, and maybe I won't."

Polly hurried over to the stable yard, where her father had parked. Bill Canfield stepped out of the cab and smiled at his daughter. He was a good-natured man in his early thirties, with blue eyes and golden hair, the same color as Polly's.

Bill Canfield took off his cap and wiped the sweat from his brow with the back of his hand. "Whew!" he said. "It sure is hot today. And it was even hotter standing in the sun at the track, watching Challenger's workout."

"Challenger must be hot, too," Polly said. "Do you want me to rub him down?"

"I rubbed him down at the track," her father said. "But you can help me get him out of the truck." He walked to the back of the truck and unfolded the ramp that was attached to the edge.

Inside the truck, Challenger stood in one of the stalls. He was a black colt with white stockings. To keep him from lurching around inside the truck, he had been hitched up to ropes attached to each side of the front of his stall.

Polly snapped the lead line onto Challenger's halter, while her father undid the ropes. Challenger began to move back and forth in anticipation of being freed, but Polly held onto his lead line. With her other hand, she patted his neck.

"Easy, boy," she said. "You'll be out of here in a minute."

After her father had finished untying the ropes, Polly took over. "Okay, boy, back up now," she said to the colt. Challenger snorted and tried to toss his head. But Polly kept a firm hold on the colt's lead line. At the same time, she slowly backed the colt out of the stall and down the ramp.

"You did a good job getting Challenger out of the truck, Polly," Bill Canfield said as he walked with her over to the colt's stall. "He's feeling pretty frisky today. I clocked him at an even forty–seven seconds. His owner is thinking of entering him in the Travers Stakes."

Polly knew that the Travers was the oldest stakes race for three-year-old horses in America. It had been run in Saratoga since 1864. A horse that won the Travers Stakes was really special.

Bill Canfield's mention of the Travers Stakes reminded Polly of her hopes for Pretty Lady. "That's swell, Dad," Polly said. "But I bet Pretty Lady could run even faster than Challenger if she had the chance. When is Mr. Harrington going to let you train her?"

James Harrington was Pretty Lady's owner. He was a rich newspaper tycoon who lived nearby on his estate. At the moment, though, he was vacationing in Europe.

Polly's father hesitated at the door to Challenger's stall. Then he turned to his daughter and said, "I'm afraid I have some bad news, Polly. Mr. Harrington sent me a telegram yesterday from London. He doesn't think Pretty Lady has it in her to win any more races. He plans to turn her into a broodmare and use her for breeding. A groom is coming here tomorrow morning to take her to the stables he's had built on his estate."

Polly stood there, unable to believe what her father had just told her.

Bill Canfield gave his daughter a sympathetic look. "I'm sorry, Polly," he said, putting his arm around her shoulders. Then he took Challenger's lead line from Polly's hand and walked the colt into his stall.

Polly felt terrible. Now Pretty Lady would never be given a chance to prove herself as a racehorse. And, even worse, after tomorrow, Pretty Lady would be gone from Canfield Farm forever.

"End of Discussion"

Before dinner, Polly and her father went out to the field to bring the horses back to the stable. When Pretty Lady and Whirlwind were the only two horses left outside, Polly said, "Please let me take Pretty Lady in, Dad. I want to spend as much time with her as I can before she goes away."

Bill Canfield turned and looked at his daughter with a surprised expression. "Are you sure?" he asked. "You know how skittish she can be."

"I think she's beginning to trust me," Polly insisted. "She let me stroke her today."

Before her father could object again, Polly walked slowly toward Pretty Lady. She talked to the filly in a soothing tone as she had done earlier, being careful to act relaxed.

When she reached Pretty Lady, she stood in front of the filly for a moment without moving a muscle. "You and I are friends, girl, remember?" she said softly.

Pretty Lady gave a snort, but once again she did not shy away from Polly's touch.

"Good girl," Polly whispered as she hitched Pretty Lady's lead line to her halter and began to lead the filly toward her father.

Bill Canfield gave a low whistle. "Well, what do you know," he said, shaking his head. "You really have a way with her, Polly."

He glanced down at his watch. "We'd better get Pretty Lady and Whirlwind settled down for the night,"

he said. "Your mother will be calling us in for dinner soon."

Polly led Pretty Lady out the gate. As she did every evening, the filly snorted nervously and pulled back when she saw the stable. She had a long memory, and the sight of the stable reminded her of the groom who had treated her so roughly. Polly soothed her with encouraging words and gentle pats, and she finally convinced Pretty Lady to step into her stall.

Despite Pretty Lady's behavior, Polly didn't feel discouraged. After what had happened between them earlier, she was sure that, with time and patience, Pretty Lady could be cured of her skittishness and retrained for racing.

"I just wish you could stay here and let Dad and me prove it," Polly said to the filly.

Just then, she heard her mother call her to dinner. Polly took one last look at Pretty Lady, who was busy nuzzling the hay net that hung from the wall. Then she closed the door of the stall and hurried over to the house.

Polly ran up the porch steps and pulled open the screen door. The door creaked as it opened and creaked again as it closed behind her. Much of the old farmhouse creaked or always seemed to be in need of repair. But it was a comfortable, friendly house, and Polly loved it.

Polly washed her hands and hurried into the dining room, where her father was ladling out servings of chicken and dumplings.

"Your father has just told me that Pretty Lady is moving to the Harringtons' stable tomorrow," Laura Canfield said. "It's too bad. She showed so much promise as a racehorse last summer. But I guess she's too skittish to race any more."

"All Pretty Lady needs is time and a patient, gentle hand," Polly insisted. "She needs you, Dad. After all, you're the best horse trainer in Saratoga."

Bill Canfield smiled at his daughter. "I'm glad you think I'm the best," he said. "But Mr. Harrington has made his decision. Now let's have dinner."

"You could talk to him about Pretty Lady," Polly said desperately. "Talk to him and try to convince him to give Pretty Lady one more chance. Please?"

Polly's father put down his fork. "I understand how sad you feel at losing Pretty Lady," he told his daughter, "but you have to understand: No matter how attached we become to the horses we stable and train here, horseracing is a business. If a Thoroughbred isn't performing, it will be sold or retired. End of discussion."

"End of Discussion"

Polly looked down at her plate in despair. Tomorrow Pretty Lady would be gone from Canfield Farm. For the rest of her days, she would be a broodmare. She would never have another chance to win a race. And there was nothing Polly could do about it.

A Secret Visit

The next morning, after Polly had helped her father feed and water the horses, she headed over to Pretty Lady's stall to turn her out into the field. As Polly was hooking the filly's lead line onto her halter, her father said, "Leave Pretty Lady in her stall. The Harringtons' groom will be arriving any minute, so there's no point in turning her out."

"I guess I'd better say goodbye to you now, then," Polly said to the filly. As she reached up and stroked Pretty Lady, her eyes filled with tears. "Goodbye, girl," she whispered in a trembling voice. "I'll miss you."

All too soon, Polly heard a truck driving up the lane. The driver, a short, gray-haired man, stepped over to Polly and her father and took off his cap. He had a pleasant, smiling face that was seamed with lines from spending many years out in the sun.

"The name's Joe McCall," he said to Polly's father. "Mr. Harrington's groom. You must be Mr. Canfield."

After the two men had shaken hands, Bill Canfield introduced Polly. Joe gave a friendly nod in Polly's direction. Then he looked over at Pretty Lady, and his face lit up with admiration. "So this is the boss's new filly," he said. "She sure is a beauty."

"Yes, she is," Bill Canfield agreed as he opened the door to Pretty Lady's stall. "But she was treated badly at another stable, and she became sour."

Joe nodded. "I know the story," he said. "It's a crying shame what some people do to horses." He reached out a hand to take Pretty Lady's lead line from Polly. Polly hesitated for a moment. Then she reluctantly handed the lead line to Joe and stepped aside so that he could lead the filly out of her stall.

Pretty Lady snorted nervously and began to pull back.

"Don't tug too hard on her line," Polly told Joe anxiously.

"Polly has grown very attached to Pretty Lady," Bill Canfield explained. "And . . ."

"And it's hard for her to see the filly go," Joe

finished. He gave Polly an understanding smile. "Don't worry, Miss," he said kindly. "I've worked with horses ever since I was a boy, and I know how to treat them. I promise to take good care of Pretty Lady. She'll have a good home."

Pretty Lady already has a good home *here*, Polly thought as she watched Joe soothe the filly and lead her up the ramp into the truck. Moments later, Polly looked on sadly as Joe drove Pretty Lady away from Canfield Farm.

Bill Canfield put his arm around his daughter's shoulders. "If you want, you can help me to train the new filly who arrived yesterday. Her name is Morning Mist. She's a little wild, and I could use your help."

"Okay, Dad," Polly said, nodding. Maybe training a new horse will help me to take my mind off Pretty Lady, she thought.

But it didn't. A little while later, as Polly stood in the center of the training ring holding the lunge rein and watching Morning Mist move in a circle around her, she couldn't help but think of Pretty Lady. She wished there were a way to see Pretty Lady and make sure she was all right.

Just then, Morning Mist tossed back her head, and Polly felt her begin to pull away. "Polly, please pay attention," her father said. "You're letting the lunge rein go slack. Tighten it up a little."

"Sorry, Dad," Polly said, pulling up on the lunge rein. Polly tried to concentrate, but her thoughts kept drifting back to Pretty Lady. She knew there was no chance that she would ever see the filly again.

Or was there? As Polly held the lunge rein and watched Morning Mist trot around the ring, she remembered that Mr. Harrington was away in Europe. She knew he had a teenage son, but he was in New York City for the summer, working as a copyboy at one of the family's newspapers. With both the Harringtons gone from the estate, she might be able to sneak in to see Pretty Lady. The more Polly thought about her idea, the better she liked it.

Later, as she was sitting at the table with her parents eating lunch, she turned to her father. "Do you need me to help you in the stable this afternoon, Dad?" she asked.

"I'll be at the track for the afternoon," her father replied, spooning a second helping of potato salad onto his plate. "So, I don't need you. I can't speak for your mother, though."

"You deserve a break, Polly," Laura Canfield said. "After all, you should be able to enjoy your summer vacation."

That was all Polly needed to hear. She hastily

swallowed the last bite of her sandwich. "May I be excused?" she asked.

"Of course," her mother said. "Have a good time."

If my plan to see Pretty Lady works, I'll have a very good time, Polly thought as she hurried out the door. As always, the screen door creaked when it was opened. "I really must oil those doors when I have the time," Polly heard her father say as the door shut behind her.

Polly ran to her bicycle, which was propped up against the side of the house. She knew that the Harringtons' estate was about a mile and a half beyond town, in an area with fields and rolling hills. Her father once had pointed out the estate to her

31

when they passed it on their way to the racetrack. Unfortunately, all she had been able to see was a long, tree-lined drive and a gate in the high, brick wall that surrounded the property.

When Polly reached the end of town, she pedaled along a quiet country road. After pedaling for several minutes, she came to the long drive of the Harringtons' estate. She rode down the drive until she reached the wrought-iron gate at the end. The drive continued past the gate and ended in a circle in front of a large, rambling, three-story clapboard house. Polly thought that her parents' little farmhouse with its small porch could have fit easily into one side of the Harringtons' mansion.

I wonder how it feels to be rich and live in a mansion like this, Polly thought as she gazed at the house beyond the gate. I bet the screen doors in this house don't creak and squeak. I bet the Harringtons have a whole army of servants to make sure everything in their house works perfectly!

She peered through the gate, trying to see where the stable was, but the large house took up her whole view. She thought for a moment, then decided to go left and follow the narrow path that ran between the woods and the high, brick wall. Polly circled the wall until she came to what she guessed was the back of the house. There the wall suddenly sloped up into an open, vine-covered archway. As Polly neared the archway, she heard a horse neigh. Polly recognized the neigh at once. It belonged to Pretty Lady.

Polly wheeled her bike through the archway and found herself in a big field. In a fenced-in area of the field, Pretty Lady fretted. She trotted nervously around the field, whinnying for the horses she had left behind at the farm.

Polly looked around anxiously to see if Joe McCall or anyone else was in sight, but except for the filly, the field seemed to be deserted. With a sigh of relief, Polly walked to the fence and, with one last look around, climbed over it.

Pretty Lady, worn out from trotting, had stopped near a section of the fence. Polly approached her, moving slowly so as not to frighten her. "Hello, girl," she said as she neared the filly. "Don't be scared. It's just me."

She stepped up to Pretty Lady and stood in front of her for a moment without moving. The filly snorted and tossed her head. She watched Polly with her usual wary look, but she did not shy away. Polly reached up and stroked her neck.

"Good girl," Polly said quietly. "You remembered that we're friends."

Polly continued to stroke Pretty Lady. She was concentrating so hard on keeping the filly calm that she was startled to hear a voice suddenly shout out, "Hey, you! What do you think you're doing with that horse?" In the next instant, a handsome, dark-haired teenage boy in knickers, boots, and a white shirt jumped down from the fence into the paddock.

The filly was startled, too. She gave a loud, high whinny and reared up. Then she turned and took off at top speed across the field, straight for the opposite fence.

Polly gasped in fear. It looked as if Pretty Lady was going to try to jump the high fence!

The Stable Boy

Pretty Lady approached the fence at a gallop. Then a few feet short of the fence the filly stopped, turned, and cantered away, snorting.

Polly whirled around and faced the boy, her eyes blazing with anger. "For crying out loud! How could you do such a thing to a horse like Pretty Lady?" she demanded. "You saw how carefully I was handling her, didn't you? For a stable hand, you obviously don't know the first thing about horses!"

"Oh, yeah?" the boy said angrily. "Well, I want to know who you are and why you're trespassing on private property!"

Polly felt the anger slide out of her. She realized

she was trespassing, and now she would have to explain herself.

"My name is Polly Canfield," she told the boy. "Pretty Lady used to be stabled at my place. Until today, that is. My father's a trainer, you see." She swallowed hard. "I know I'm trespassing, but I really had to see Pretty Lady again. We were just starting to become friends before she had to go away to live here."

The boy's expression softened as he listened to Polly. "Gee, that's tough," he said in a sympathetic tone. "I know how I'd feel if I lost a horse I cared about." He paused for a moment. "My name's Mike, by the way."

Polly nodded and turned her attention back to Pretty Lady. The filly was standing across the field looking over the fence. Mike followed Polly's gaze.

"She's one of the niftiest Thoroughbreds I've ever seen," Mike said admiringly. "And one of the fastest, too. I've never seen a filly move as speedily as she just did."

They watched Pretty Lady in silence for a moment. Then Mike turned to Polly. "Say, I'm sorry I shouted at you before," he said. "I guess I got a little carried away when I saw a trespasser on the property. How did you get in here, anyway?"

Polly pointed to the brick wall. "I came in through the archway in the wall," she explained. "I didn't see anyone around, so I thought it would be safe to visit Pretty Lady."

"I'm really sorry I spooked her," Mike said. "I just arrived here this afternoon, and I haven't had a chance to meet the horses yet. I didn't realize Pretty Lady would react like that. What has made her so nervous, anyway?"

Polly told him about Pretty Lady's promising career, the bad stable, and the groom's rough handling of the filly. When she described some of the bad treatment Pretty Lady had received, she saw Mike's face darken with anger.

Polly felt glad that Mike shared her outrage at what had happened to Pretty Lady.

She looked across the field at the filly. Pretty Lady was still standing by the fence. Every so often, she tossed her head and snorted nervously. "Pretty Lady is still jittery," Polly said. "I can tell."

"It's time to bring her in," Mike said. He climbed over the fence and ran off toward a long, white building. A few moments later he was back, holding Pretty Lady's halter. He started toward the filly.

"Wait a minute," Polly said quickly.

Mike stopped, turned, and gave her a questioning

look. "What's the matter?" he asked.

"I think you should let me bring her in," Polly said. "You might be the stable boy here, but I know Pretty Lady better than you do. She trusts me."

An amused smile crossed Mike's face.

I bet he thinks I can't do it, Polly thought. "What's so funny?" she asked him in a huffy tone.

"Oh, nothing," Mike replied. "It's just that I . . ." He paused for a moment. Then he shook his head and said, "Never mind." He gestured toward Pretty Lady. "Go ahead, see if you can get her. For a kid, you seem pretty sure of yourself."

"I'm not a kid," Polly said hotly. "I'm twelve going on thirteen. How old are *you*, anyway?"

"I turned fifteen last month," Mike replied.

"Oh," Polly said. "Well, I don't care if you are older than I am. Like I told you, I know Pretty Lady. You don't. Just watch me bring her in." She took the halter from him. Then, without another word, she turned and walked off across the field toward the filly.

In her determination to show Mike that she knew how to handle Pretty Lady, she forgot to approach the filly slowly and quietly. As soon as Pretty Lady saw Polly coming, she shook her head and backed away.

.Polly slowed her stride and carefully moved toward Pretty Lady again. This time she managed to step up to the filly. "That's right, girl," she said gently. "You know you can trust me."

She reached out her hand toward Pretty Lady. As soon as the filly felt the touch of Polly's hand, her nostrils flared and she pinned back her ears. Then she tossed her head, turned, and twisted away. Polly ran in front of her to block her retreat, but Pretty Lady turned away from her again.

"Come on, girl," Polly said desperately. "Stop acting so skittish. We're supposed to be friends, remember?"

She approached Pretty Lady, and once again the filly twisted away. Try as she might, Polly could not convince Pretty Lady to settle down. Finally, Polly gave up.

Discouraged, she walked back to Mike. He was standing with his back against the fence, his arms folded across his chest. There was a thoughtful look in his eyes and a smile on his handsome face.

He'd better not laugh at me, Polly thought furiously. He'd better not say I'm just a kid who doesn't know how to handle a skittish horse.

But Mike didn't say a word to Polly. Instead, he took the halter from her, moved away from the fence, and walked toward Pretty Lady.

"All right, girl," Polly heard him say in a soothing

murmur as he walked. "No one's going to hurt you. Calm down."

As Polly watched Mike, she was surprised to see that he had closed one of his eyes. What's he doing that for? Polly wondered.

She also noticed that Pretty Lady did not shy when she saw the stable boy approach her. To Polly's amazement, the filly stood completely still and let Mike step right up to her and slip on her halter.

It won't last, Polly thought smugly. In another minute, Pretty Lady will twist out of his grasp and run away from him, just like she ran away from me.

But Polly was wrong. Several minutes passed, and Pretty Lady still stood calmly in the same spot. Even when Mike released his hold on her halter, Pretty Lady continued to stand quietly and let him stroke her.

Polly couldn't stand it any longer. She had to know what Mike had done to make Pretty Lady calm down like that. She started to head toward them. At the same time, Mike walked toward her, leading Pretty Lady by the halter. The filly jerked her head up and down several times, but she followed him obediently without trying to pull away.

"How did you do that?" Polly asked Mike, when he and the filly had reached her. "Was it some kind of trick?"

41

"That's exactly what it was," Mike said with a grin. "It's the one-eye trick. I learned it from my grandfather, my father's father. He was a horse trainer in Ireland and a good one, too. He taught me everything he knew about horses."

Polly took advantage of the fact that Pretty Lady was standing close to her, and she gently stroked the filly's neck. "Tell me more about the one-eye trick."

"Why don't I explain it while we walk Pretty Lady over to the stable," Mike suggested. "She's had enough excitement for one day. Besides," he added with a smile, "I bet you want to see our stable to make sure that Pretty Lady is living in comfort."

Polly noticed that Mike had a very nice smile that lit up his whole face. She smiled back at him and nodded. "You're right," she said eagerly. "I would like to see where Pretty Lady is living."

Polly walked next to Pretty Lady as Mike led the filly through the gate. "The one-eye trick is pretty simple," Mike continued, as they approached the stable. "You walk toward the horse slowly but confidently, but with one eye closed. The horse is caught off guard and doesn't have time to react. It can be a good way to calm down a nervous horse, like Pretty Lady."

They had reached the long, freshly painted white

42

building. A string of stalls stretched from one end of the stable to the other, similar to the stalls at Canfield Farm.

"The stable is brand new," Mike told her. "Right now we have only five horses, but by next summer, every stall should be filled." He led Pretty Lady over to an end stall. Polly opened the door so that Mike could walk the filly inside. She glanced into the stall and saw that there was fresh straw on the floor, a water pail, and a hay net. Everything looked neat, clean, and comfortable.

Once inside, Pretty Lady turned and poked her head over the top of the Dutch door. Mike pulled a lump of sugar from his pocket and gave it to the filly, along with a pat on her neck. Pretty Lady ate the sugar lump daintily. Polly saw how gentle Mike was with Pretty Lady and how the filly was beginning to trust him. Her neck was arched and her ears were pricked forward, which meant she was feeling relaxed and friendly.

"Well, I guess I'd better go home now," Polly said reluctantly. "It's getting late. Anyway, you probably have work to do."

"I'll take extra-good care of Pretty Lady," Mike promised her. "And you can visit her any time you want. But next time, come to the gate, ring the bell, and I'll let you in. There are two bells on the wall by the gate. The bottom bell rings in the stable."

Polly nodded. "I'll remember," she said. "And thanks, Mike." A doorbell that rings in the stable! she thought. The Harringtons really must be rich if they have something like that!

She reached up to give Pretty Lady a loving pat. "Goodbye, girl," she whispered. "I'll see you again soon."

As she was riding home on her bike, Polly decided that Mike was a very nice boy. She remembered how gentle he was with Pretty Lady, and she felt reassured that he would keep his promise to treat the filly with extra-special care. And best of all, she could visit Pretty Lady every day if she wanted to!

Everything would be just about perfect, Polly thought, if only Mr. Harrington could be convinced to give Pretty Lady another chance to race.

CHAPTER
SIX

New Plans

The next time Polly went to see Pretty Lady, she rang the bottom bell by the front gate, as Mike had suggested. She waited for several moments, but Mike did not appear. Just as she was beginning to worry that he either hadn't heard the bell ring in the stable or wasn't on the estate, she saw him hurrying toward her.

"I'm glad you decided to come back to visit Pretty Lady," Mike said with a smile as he walked up to the gate. "She's waiting for you." He reached into the pocket of his knickers and pulled out a set of keys. He selected a large key from the ring, unlocked the gate, and pulled it open.

I'm glad that I'm a guest on the estate today and not a trespasser, Polly thought, as she stepped through the gate. Even if I am just a guest of the Harringtons' stable boy.

"I'm sorry I took so long to get here," Mike said, closing the gate behind her. "I was using the phone in the stable office to call the vet. One of the mares has developed a bad case of colic. Joe's with her now."

"Gee, you have a phone in the stable office," Polly said with awe.

Mike looked at her in surprise. "Doesn't your father have a phone in his office?" he asked.

"Dad doesn't even have an office," Polly replied with a laugh. "When he needs to write bills or pay them, he uses the kitchen table as a desk.

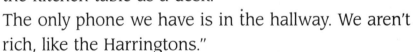

The only phone we have is in the hallway. We aren't rich, like the Harringtons."

They were walking around the raked gravel drive in front of the house. Polly gazed around her in awe. Now that she was closer to the house, Polly could see more clearly how beautiful the mansion and the carefully landscaped grounds around it really were.

The front door of the house was made of polished oak, and there was a gleaming brass knocker in the center of it. There were flower boxes and brightly striped awnings at each of the mansion's windows, and expensive-looking white wicker sofas, chairs, and tables on the verandas.

When Polly and Mike reached the back of the house, Polly saw a huge stone patio with wide steps that led down to a marble fountain. The fountain had three levels. Water flowed in a stream from the top level to a fish pond at the bottom of the fountain. On another part of the lawn was a swimming pool surrounded by a tiled patio.

Polly gazed around her with shining eyes. "The Harringtons' estate is so beautiful," she said with a sigh as they walked through a tall hedge that separated the back lawn from the field and the stable. "It must be wonderful to be rich. I bet that Mr. Harrington's son gets anything he wants."

Mike shrugged. "Being rich isn't so swell, I bet," he said. "I'd rather work with horses any day than be rich."

Polly noticed a bitter tone in Mike's voice, and she wondered why it was there. Maybe deep down he wished that he were rich, too.

"Well, I think it would be nifty to work with horses and be rich," Polly said. "But I know what you mean. Anyway, I bet Mr. Harrington's son is really spoiled."

Just then, Polly spotted Pretty Lady standing in the fenced-in field, and her eyes lit up with pleasure.

"I have to go back to the stable now to wait for the vet to arrive," Mike told her. "But I'll come over as soon as he's finished treating the mare. Do you mind?"

Polly shook her head. She didn't mind at all. She felt glad at the chance to have Pretty Lady all to herself. Mike smiled at her and hurried off toward the stable. At the same time, Polly eagerly headed toward the field.

Pretty Lady had been drinking from a small pond in the middle of the field. Now she wandered over to a corner section of the fence near the gate. Polly circled the fence to where Pretty Lady was standing and stepped up to the filly. When Pretty Lady saw Polly, she nickered softly.

"Hello, girl," Polly said. "I see you're feeling friendlier today." She carefully climbed up onto the bottom rung of the fence, slowly reached out her hand, and gently stroked the filly's neck. "I guess you're getting used to your new home."

The thought that Pretty Lady liked living here as much as she had liked living at Canfield Farm made Polly feel a little sad. But she noticed that the filly looked healthy, well-groomed, and relaxed, and she had to admit that Mike had kept his promise to look after her.

I still wish she were living with us, Polly thought. But she seems happy and contented, and that's what matters.

As she stroked Pretty Lady, Polly noticed a cavesson, lunge line, and lunge whip near the gate. Impulsively, she decided to see how Pretty Lady would respond to the lunge line. Polly knew that if she were training the filly, she would start with lunging exercises to teach her to obey human commands again. The exercises would also help to calm and strengthen Pretty Lady and to make her more supple.

Polly patted the filly and said, "Don't go away, girl. I'll be right back." She walked over to the gate, picked up the tack, and slowly approached Pretty Lady. When she reached the filly, she slipped the cavesson over her head and clipped the lunge line onto the metal ring in the center of the cavesson.

"Good girl," Polly said in an approving tone. She patted the filly. "Now that didn't hurt a bit, did it?"

Pretty Lady shook her head and gave a snort. She

didn't seem to mind wearing the cavesson, but her behavior showed Polly that she was beginning to feel restless.

"First, we'll try a walk," Polly said to the filly. She held the lunge line in her left hand and pulled gently on it. Pretty Lady snorted and tried to jerk away from Polly's grasp. Polly tugged the line again. This time the filly did not pull back. Instead, she stood stubbornly where she was. Try as she might, Polly could not get her to budge. It was as if Pretty Lady were made of stone.

Polly loosened her grip on the lunge line and began to stroke the filly's neck. "Please take a walk with me, girl," she said softly. "Just a short walk, okay?"

Polly patiently continued to stroke Pretty Lady and to talk to her in soothing tones. At the same time, she pulled gently on the lunge line. Finally, to Polly's relief, the filly moved forward. Polly led Pretty Lady into the center of a small ring she had noticed earlier and walked her around in a circle. After they had completed the circle, Polly stopped and said, "Halt." The filly stopped moving.

I knew she would remember how to respond to commands, Polly thought excitedly.

She smiled at Pretty Lady. "Good girl," she said. "I

knew you could do it. Now, let's try it again."

This time, as Polly circled the ring with Pretty Lady, she let the lunge line out slowly, until she was standing several feet away from Pretty Lady, and the filly was moving counterclockwise around her.

Polly knew that using the lunge whip would scare Pretty Lady. Instead she relied on her voice and the firm but gentle repetition of the commands, "Walk" and "Halt," to make the filly obey her.

At first, Pretty Lady responded to Polly's commands, but she soon felt the freedom of being held so loosely on the lunge line, and she turned away from Polly and quickly doubled back to the outside of the circle.

Just then, Polly spotted Mike walking toward the ring. All of a sudden, she felt uneasy about what she had done. She realized that Mike might very well be angry with her for taking Pretty Lady out of the field and using the lunging tack without permission.

Polly pulled on the lunge line and told the filly to halt. Pretty Lady snorted and stopped in her tracks. Polly quickly unclipped the lunge line and removed the cavesson. The filly shook her head and then immediately trotted away to the other side of the ring. Polly turned to face Mike, who was entering the ring.

"I saw the tack, and I thought I'd see if Pretty

Lady would respond to some lunging exercises," Polly explained in a rush as Mike stepped over to her. "I think that she could be a winner again. All she needs is a gentle hand and some retraining."

She stopped and waited anxiously for Mike to reply. To her relief, he smiled at her and said, "I agree. Yesterday, when I saw Pretty Lady galloping across the field, I felt that she had the mark of a true champion."

Without thinking, Polly and Mike had begun to walk together across the ring to where Pretty Lady was standing. When they reached the filly, Mike picked up the lunge line and cavesson Polly had left on the ground.

All of a sudden, Polly stared at Mike, her eyes wide. "That tack," she said. *"You're* the one who left it there!"

Mike nodded. "I was going to try some lunging exercises with Pretty Lady today, too," he admitted. He hesitated for a moment. Then he said almost shyly, "See, my dream has always been to become a professional horse trainer, like my grandfather. And I want to train Thoroughbred racehorses, like he did. When you told me about Pretty Lady, I thought that she was getting a raw deal," Mike continued. "She deserves a second chance to race, and I want to give her that chance. My plan is to train her and then convince Mr. Harrington to enter her in the Travers Stakes."

"Gee, Mike, that's swell," Polly said, looking at him with shining eyes. "We can work together!"

"Well, I don't know about that," Mike said with a frown. "Training Pretty Lady to race in the Travers Stakes means a lot to me. What do you know about training horses? You're just a kid."

Polly turned to him, her face flushed with anger. "For crying out loud, stop calling me a *kid*!" she said hotly. "Anyway, I bet I know just as much as you do about training horses. My father is a professional trainer, and he's taught me, just as your grandfather taught you."

Mike studied her thoughtfully. Then he shook his head. "I don't know, Polly," he said doubtfully. "I saw you earlier with Pretty Lady. It looked like you were having a hard time controlling her."

"But that's just because it was her first time on the lunge," Polly argued.

"Maybe that's true," Mike admitted. "But for now, I'm going to train her myself." He walked back to Pretty Lady and slipped on her cavesson.

Polly felt her eyes fill with tears of frustration as she watched Mike clip the lunge line onto Pretty Lady's cavesson. It was my idea to train Pretty Lady in the first place! she thought angrily. And now Mike is taking over. He's just a stable boy, but he acts as if Pretty Lady belongs to him.

Polly brushed the tears from her eyes, turned, and began to march out of the ring. When she reached the gate, she stopped in her tracks. She was still angry at Mike, but she was also curious to see what kind of a trainer he was and how well Pretty Lady would obey his commands.

Polly climbed up onto the fence and sat on the top rail. She watched as Mike let out the lunge line and said in an encouraging tone, "Okay, girl, walk now." Pretty Lady shook her head, snorted, and stayed where she was. Mike repeated the command. This time, Pretty Lady stepped forward. Then she turned toward Mike and walked in the opposite direction from where he wanted her to go.

Polly stifled a giggle. "You'll never get her to obey you that way," she called out.

"Huh?" Mike said, turning toward her. "What do you mean?"

"Here," Polly said, climbing down from the fence and walking over to him. "Give me the lunge line, and I'll show you."

She held out her hand. Mike hesitated for a moment. Then he shrugged and gave it to her. "Pretty

Lady is skittish, remember?" she said to him as she looped up the lunge line and held it so that she was standing close to the filly. "She'll act up if you let her. You can't give her freedom on the lunge right at the beginning, and you can't hurry her. You have to remind her of what she's supposed to do first."

Polly led Pretty Lady around in a small, counterclockwise circle. She talked to the filly in soothing tones as they walked. After Polly and Pretty Lady had completed two circles, Polly let out the lunge line. Soon she was standing in the center of the ring, and Pretty Lady was circling around her. Polly was pleased to see how well Pretty Lady responded to her calm but firm commands to walk and halt.

Smiling, she turned to look at Mike. "Well?" she asked, trying hard not to sound smug. "How did I do?"

Mike shook his head with admiration. "I thought you were spouting a lot of banana oil before, when you told me you knew how to train horses," he told her. "But you really showed me up just now."

He walked over to Polly and held out his hand. "I guess that means we're going to be partners after all," he said.

Polly shook Mike's hand. "I guess it does," she replied. "When do you want to meet again?" she asked eagerly.

"The sooner the better," Mike replied. "How about tomorrow afternoon, after lunch?"

Polly nodded in agreement. "That would be perfect," she said, adding, "Maybe we should take Pretty Lady back to the field now. She'd probably like some freedom after all that hard work."

"Would you mind doing it?" Mike asked. "I'd like to check on the colicky mare."

"I don't mind," Polly said with a smile. She led the filly out of the ring.

When she reached the field, she led Pretty Lady through the gate. She unclipped the lunge line and slipped off the cavesson.

"Congratulations, girl," she whispered. "You just took the first step into the winner's circle!"

CHAPTER SEVEN

Becoming a Team

Every afternoon Polly and Mike worked hard to train Pretty Lady. They kept her on the lunge, and slowly but surely, they convinced her to trot and canter, as well as to walk, around the ring. One day Polly held the lunge line and gave the commands; the next day, Mike did. Polly was glad they were taking turns and working as a team. At first she had been a little worried that Mike would try to take over because he was older than she was.

Now that Pretty Lady was in training, Polly and Mike kept her apart from the other horses. She was turned out for only a few hours each day. As the weeks went by, Pretty Lady became calmer, stronger, and more supple. But the filly could still be difficult at times. One hot July afternoon, as Polly was holding two lunge reins and walking behind Pretty Lady while the filly circled the ring, she heard a low rumble of thunder in the distance. Without thinking, Polly looked up at the sky and saw dark clouds beginning to form.

Suddenly, she felt Pretty Lady turn sharply to the left and saw her move her hindquarters to the right. "Polly, you're holding her inside line too tightly," she heard Mike say. "You're throwing her off balance."

"Sorry," Polly said, immediately slackening the inside line so that it was the same length as the outside line. But Pretty Lady had been distracted by Polly's mistake. She gave a snort, shook her head, and stopped halfway around the circle.

"Walk, girl," Polly ordered. Pretty Lady refused to budge.

Mike stepped over to Pretty Lady. "What's wrong?" he asked the filly softly as he stroked her. "I made a mistake with the lunge line yesterday, and you didn't let it bother you."

Just then there was another low rumble of thunder. Pretty Lady whinnied. "Is the thunder making you nervous?" Mike asked.

Polly smiled as she watched the stable boy soothe

Pretty Lady. At first, all Mike had seemed to care about was training the filly to be a prizewinning racehorse. But as the weeks went on, Polly noticed a change in the way Mike handled Pretty Lady. Slowly he seemed to be learning to like the filly for herself, not just because she might win an important race. Polly was glad that he liked Pretty Lady almost as much as she herself did.

It thundered again, and the wind picked up. Polly felt a few drops of rain. "It's going to rain hard any minute," Polly said. "We should take Pretty Lady back to the stable until the storm is over."

Mike nodded and led the filly out of the ring. Pretty Lady balked once, then followed him. Polly could tell from the way she snorted and tossed her head that Pretty Lady was feeling nervous.

As they walked toward the stable, Polly glanced at the field and saw Joe McCall bringing in the Thoroughbred mare who had been sick with colic a few weeks ago. The Harringtons' three other horses still grazed and didn't seem to be at all nervous at the approaching storm, but Polly knew that they would have to be brought to shelter. She looked at Mike and was surprised that he made no move to help Joe.

"Shouldn't you help Joe bring in the horses?" Polly asked Mike. "Isn't that part of your job?"

"My job?" Mike said, looking at her with a puzzled expression. "Oh, yes . . . sure, that's my job."

He handed Pretty Lady's lunge reins to Polly and hurried off toward the field. Polly looked after him and shook her head. "I guess Mike likes you so much, he's forgotten about the other horses around here," she said to Pretty Lady as she continued walking the filly back to the stable.

The rain began to pour just as Polly led Pretty Lady into her stall. Polly could tell from the filly's relaxed behavior that she was relieved to be safe inside. Polly checked her water supply, then stepped out of the stall and stood under the overhang, waiting for the storm to end.

A moment later, she saw Mike walk toward the stable, leading a dark bay mare. Behind him was Joe with a dappled gray mare. It continued to thunder, and Polly could hear the rain beat down on the roof of the stable.

"Thanks for your help, Mr. Mike," she heard Joe say as he passed Mike on his way to the gray mare's stall. "I'll go and get the other mare." Polly noticed the respectful tone in Joe's voice, and she wondered at it. She also didn't understand why Joe had called his stable boy "Mister." Maybe it was some kind of joke between them.

After several minutes, Mike came out of the bay mare's stall and joined Polly under the overhang. "What a storm," he said as a gust of wind blew a sheet of rain into their faces. "It's a good thing we got the horses in when we did. And ourselves, too. I remember being in the middle of Central Park in New York City once, when a storm like this began. The guy I was riding with wouldn't go back to the stable. He nearly got both of us struck by lightning."

This was the first time Mike had ever talked about himself. Polly suddenly realized that even though she had been working with him for three weeks, she really knew very little about him. They had been so busy training Pretty Lady, they hadn't had a chance to talk about themselves. Polly didn't know who Mike's family was or where he came from. She didn't even know the Harringtons' stable boy's last name.

"New York City? Is that where you lived before you came to Saratoga?" she asked Mike.

Mike nodded. Polly waited for him to say more, but he didn't. So she asked, "Do you have any brothers or sisters?"

"No," Mike said briefly. "I'm an only child."

"I am, too," Polly said. "Most of the time I like it that way. But sometimes I wish I had a brother or a sister. Then Mother and Dad wouldn't expect so much from me. Sometimes they treat me like an adult. But other times, they act as if I'm too young to make my own decisions."

Mike looked at her with interest. Then he stared at the rain and said, "I think I know what you mean."

Polly wondered why he sounded so sad. "Did your parents mind when you decided to come to Saratoga to work?" she asked.

"They didn't say anything about it," Mike said. "They couldn't." Before Polly could say anything else, he added quickly, "The rain's stopped, but the ground will be too wet to take Pretty Lady out for more lunge work. Why don't we just call it a day until tomorrow?"

"Sure," Polly said. She sensed that Mike didn't want to talk about his parents, though she didn't understand why.

As Polly rode home, she went over in her mind the conversation with Mike. Maybe he didn't have a family anymore. Maybe they had died and now he was an orphan. She decided that she would never ask him about his parents again. She was sure that it hurt Mike too much to talk about them.

The First Ride

One afternoon in late July, after Mike had let Polly in through the front gate, he said to her, "The Travers Stakes is just a few weeks away, and Mr. Harrington is due back any day. That means we don't have much time left. Pretty Lady's been making such good progress on the lunge. Maybe we should try and saddle her."

Polly's eyes lit up. For several days now, she had been thinking the same thing. "That's a swell idea," she said eagerly. "First we should lunge her with the riding tack. Then, if she lets us ride her, we can start working on her speed."

They stopped at the tack room at the end of the

stable to get the lunging tack. Then they picked out a bridle, a saddle, and a saddle pad. Polly also took a martingale off one of the hooks on the wall. "We'll need this to keep Pretty Lady from tossing her head up during the ride," Polly said.

They carried the tack over to the small ring and then went over to the field to get Pretty Lady. "Let's keep her as calm as possible," Polly suggested as they approached the filly. "She's been pretty relaxed lately, but we don't know how she's going to react to the bridle and the saddle."

Slowly they stepped over to Pretty Lady. Polly slipped the lunging cavesson over her head. "So far, so good," Polly whispered to Mike as the filly obediently followed her on the lunge line.

After Polly had led Pretty Lady into the ring, Mike brought the bridle over to the filly. "You remember this," he said as he placed the bit in her mouth. Pretty Lady jerked her head up as she felt the bit go in, but she didn't shy away, and Mike was able to slip the bridle over her head. Polly snapped on the lunge line and held it firmly as Mike placed the martingale around the filly's neck.

Next Mike placed the saddle pad on Pretty Lady's back. "Here comes the tricky part," he murmured as he picked up the saddle. He brought the saddle over to the filly and lifted it up to put it on her back. Pretty Lady snorted and pranced back and forth. Mike lowered the saddle and held it until the filly had stopped prancing.

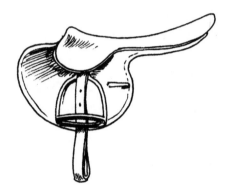

Polly stroked the filly. As soon as she touched Pretty Lady, she felt the filly tremble. "No one's going to hurt you, girl," Polly said softly. "I promise."

As Polly stroked Pretty Lady, Mike lifted up the saddle again. This time, Pretty Lady stood still while he placed it on her back. He slid the end of the martingale onto the girth strap, buckled the girth, and stood up. Pretty Lady snorted and shook her head several times.

Using the lunge line, Polly walked Pretty Lady around the ring. Then she let out the line and lunged the filly counterclockwise around her.

"I think she's gotten used to wearing the riding tack," Polly said, after the filly had circled several times. "Now we should lunge her with a rider. It's been a long time since she's had the weight of a rider on her back, and she needs to get used to it again."

"Okay, Pretty Lady," Mike said, stepping up to the filly. "Let's see if you'll agree to let me sit on your back."

Polly bent over and laced her fingers together to give Mike a leg up. Mike put his foot into Polly's hands and hoisted himself up onto Pretty Lady's back. As soon as the filly felt Mike's weight on her back, she whinnied and pranced nervously. Polly quickly stepped away.

Pretty Lady whinnied again and reared, throwing Mike to the ground. Polly rushed over to him. "Are you all right?" she asked anxiously.

Mike sat up and slowly shook his head. "I'm fine," he said a bit breathlessly. "I just had the wind knocked out of me."

"Let me try," Polly said, handing him the lunge line. Mike gave her a leg up, and she hoisted herself into the saddle.

Pretty Lady pranced again, but Mike kept a firm hold on the lunge line, and the filly was unable to rear.

"Calm down, now, girl," Polly said. She continued to talk to Pretty Lady quietly, and the filly finally stood still.

"I'm going to lunge her," Mike said. Polly nodded and held onto the reins as Mike let out the lunge line.

"Walk on, girl," Mike commanded. The filly shook her head and refused to go forward. Oh, no, Polly thought. She's balking again.

"Walk on," Mike repeated calmly but firmly. This time, Pretty Lady stepped forward. Polly glanced over at Mike, and they smiled at each other. Polly was sure he was thinking the same thing she was. If Pretty Lady had gotten over her habit of balking under saddle, it meant that their training was really working.

"Would you like to take over?" Mike asked after awhile.

"Very much," Polly said, nodding. She held the reins firmly and used her hands and her voice to command Pretty Lady to circle several times around Mike. Then Mike unclipped the lunge line, and Polly said, "Halt."

The filly stopped. Polly touched her boots to the filly's sides and clicked her tongue against the roof of her mouth. Pretty Lady hesitated for a moment, and Polly repeated the signals. The filly started forward.

After Polly had commanded Pretty Lady to walk and trot around the ring several times, she urged the filly into a canter. Pretty Lady moved into the faster gait with high-spirited ease. Polly sensed that the filly wanted to go even faster, so she called out to Mike, "I want to take her for a run."

"Are you sure?" Mike asked.

"I'm sure," Polly replied with a confident smile. She gripped the reins and guided Pretty Lady out of the ring. When they had cantered past the fenced-in field, Polly urged the filly into a gallop. Pretty Lady was only too happy to obey.

Polly felt wonderful galloping across the field. She had ridden Thoroughbreds before, to exercise them, but none of them had been as fast as Pretty Lady. Polly could have galloped forever, but she knew she shouldn't tire the filly out.

"Whoa, girl," she called as she pulled on the reins. At first the high-spirited filly refused to stop, but Polly continued to pull on the reins, and the filly finally slowed to a canter.

"Right now, you need a rubdown and a drink of water," Polly told Pretty Lady as she guided the filly toward the stable at a walk.

"Mike and I were right about you all along, girl," she said softly. "I can't wait to show you to Mr. Harrington. After he sees how fast you are, I just know he'll want to enter you in the Travers Stakes!"

A Party

For the next few weeks, Polly and Mike took turns riding Pretty Lady. Soon they were galloping the filly on the estate's practice track, using a stopwatch to mark her time. They conditioned her legs with long gallops and began to ask her for bursts of speed as she rounded the track. Polly and Mike knew that the filly would need to speed up quickly at the start of the race.

One day, as Polly and Mike were examining Pretty Lady's legs for signs of swelling, Polly said, "It's so quiet here. I'm worried that Pretty Lady will become nervous again when we take her to the track. There will be a lot of noise and people around."

Mike nodded and thought for a minute. "I'll be right back," he said, running off toward the stable office. Several moments later, he was back, lugging a phonograph.

"This belongs to Joe," Mike said with a grin. "We can use it to see how Pretty Lady reacts to the sound."

Mike cranked up the phonograph and started to play a record, a loud, boisterous marching tune.

Pretty Lady snorted and shook her head, but she didn't skitter.

"I don't think she likes the music very much," Polly said with a laugh.

"As long as the sound doesn't bother her, that's all that matters," Mike said, smiling.

Every day after that, Mike played the phonograph during Pretty Lady's workout. The filly soon became accustomed to the sound of Joe's records as she galloped around the track.

As Pretty Lady's workouts continued, her time improved. Polly and Mike were pleased with the filly's progress, but they also began to feel that she needed a break from her training.

"Why don't we take Pretty Lady for a longer ride today?" Mike suggested late one afternoon, after Polly had galloped Pretty Lady around the track. "There's a big field on the other side of the estate. I rode the bay mare over there this morning."

"Swell," Polly said. She gave the filly a pat, adding, "I bet Pretty Lady would like a nice, long, easy ride, wouldn't you, girl?" The filly tossed her head and neighed. Polly was sure she was eager to be off.

They decided that Mike would ride Pretty Lady to the field, and Polly would ride the gray mare. On the way back, they would switch.

They quickly saddled up the two horses and set off. As they cantered across the Harringtons' field, Polly couldn't help but notice the difference between the horse she was riding and Pretty Lady. The gray mare was sweet-tempered and speedy, but she wasn't half as fast as the filly, or as exciting to ride.

Soon they were cantering across the next field side by side. "It's beautiful here," Polly said, gazing around at the brightly colored wildflowers that covered the field.

Mike motioned toward a gently sloping hill up ahead. "On the other side of that hill is a pond. We can rest the horses there before we ride back."

Polly nodded and urged the mare on. As she began to climb the hill, Mike and Pretty Lady passed her. Mike grinned at Polly over his shoulder. What a couple of showoffs, Polly thought, smiling.

After Polly had ridden down the other side of the hill, she brought the mare to a halt in front of a small pond ringed with fir trees. Mike had already dismounted, and Polly did the same.

"You and Pretty Lady were cantering faster than we were. I couldn't keep up," Polly said to Mike as she slipped the reins over the mare's head. Together, she and Mike led the horses down to the edge of the pond for a drink. Pretty Lady and the mare both slurped up the clear water noisily.

"Pretty Lady was born to go fast," Mike said. "That's why she's going to win the Travers Stakes."

Polly looked over at him. "Winning the race

means a lot to you, doesn't it?" she asked. "I remember you saying that the day we started to train Pretty Lady together."

Mike nodded. "It *is* important to me," he admitted. "If she wins, I'll be closer to my dream of becoming a professional horse trainer."

"Oh," Polly said in a low tone. "I guess you wish you had trained Pretty Lady alone. Then you could take all the credit when she wins the race."

Mike smiled and shook his head. "No, Polly, you're wrong," he said. "I thought that at first, but I realized very soon that I couldn't train Pretty Lady without you. We'll both share the credit when she wins. We're a team, remember?"

Polly and Mike stood together in comfortable silence for a moment, looking out across the pond. Suddenly, Polly noticed that the sun was getting lower in the sky. "Say, we'd better start back before it gets dark," she said to Mike.

They quickly led the horses away from the water. Polly mounted Pretty Lady and urged her back up the hill. Mike, on the gray mare, followed behind. As Polly guided Pretty Lady toward the field, she felt how responsive the filly was to her slightest command. A month ago, she was a sour horse, Polly thought as she urged the filly into a gallop. Now she's confident and high-spirited, just as she should be.

The sun was setting by the time Polly and Mike reached the Harringtons' field. They slowed the horses to a walk, and as they came closer to the house, Polly was surprised to hear the sounds of a jazz band coming from the patio. She stopped Pretty Lady and looked toward the house. Expensive-looking cars were driving up to the front of the house. Men in tuxedos and women in stylish evening dresses climbed out of the cars.

Polly looked at the patio and saw that it was lit by strings of multicolored Chinese lanterns. A crowd of men and women milled around the patio and stood by the big fountain on the back lawn, talking and laughing. Through the crowd servants with trays passed, offering food and drinks.

The band began to play a Charleston. Many couples immediately stopped talking and laughing and began to dance. Polly watched the beads on the women's dresses glitter in the lantern light. The silky ostrich feathers waved in their hair as they moved their arms and legs to the rhythm of the dance.

"Gee," Polly said in an awed tone as she gazed with wide, admiring eyes at the scene before her. "I knew people gave ritzy parties like this in Saratoga, but I've never actually seen one until now."

She turned to Mike. "The party must mean that Mr. Harrington has come home," she said excitedly. "Now you can tell him about Pretty Lady."

When Mike didn't reply, Polly looked at him more closely. She was surprised to see that he was pale and that he had a grim expression on his face. She was even more surprised when he said urgently, "We have to get the horses back to the stable right now, Polly. Before Mr. Harrington sees us."

Quickly Mike dismounted, slipped the reins over the gray mare's head, and began to lead her away.

Polly stared at Mike for a moment with a puzzled expression. Then she climbed off Pretty Lady and followed him with the filly. They led the horses around the edge of the crowd toward the stable. As they came closer to the party, Polly hoped Pretty Lady would stay calm with all the people and noise around her.

To Polly's relief, the filly followed her quietly. Then, just as they were passing the fountain, Polly saw a woman with bright red lips look over at them. "Ooh!" the woman squealed with delight when she noticed Pretty Lady. "What a nifty-looking horse!" She motioned to a few of her friends, who were standing nearby. "Come on over, everybody, and see the pretty horse!"

Before Polly could lead Pretty Lady away, the woman and her friends rushed up to the filly and began to pat her. Pretty Lady snorted and nervously backed away.

"Please don't crowd her," Polly begged the woman and her friends as she struggled to control the skittish filly. "Can't you see that you're making her nervous?"

But they didn't pay any attention to Polly's plea. They went on patting Pretty Lady and exclaiming over her beauty. Their continual fussing made the filly more and more nervous. She jerked up her head and started to rear. Polly gripped the reins tightly and managed to turn the filly away from the woman and her friends. She talked to Pretty Lady in soothing tones and kept a firm, close hold on the reins as she led the frightened filly toward the stable.

"Well, how do you like that!" she heard one of the women say indignantly. "What's wrong with that horse, anyway?"

An Unpleasant Meeting

When Polly led Pretty Lady into her stall and removed her saddle and bridle, she could see that the filly was still nervous. Pretty Lady snorted and shook her head and pranced back and forth in the stall. "I'm sorry those people scared you like that, girl," Polly said softly.

Polly knew Pretty Lady needed a rubdown after her trip to the field, but the filly was acting so skittish that she decided to leave her alone for a while.

She stepped out of the stall and saw Mike coming toward her from the gray mare's stall. "What took you so long?" he asked in a worried tone. "You didn't run into Mr. Harrington, did you?"

"No," Polly said. She explained to him what had happened. "Pretty Lady is still skittish," she finished. "I certainly hope we can calm her down by the time Mr. Harrington sees her." She paused for a moment. Then she said, "I don't understand something, Mike. Why didn't you want Mr. Harrington to see us?"

"I didn't want to interrupt the Harringtons' swanky party, that's all," Mike muttered.

"Oh," Polly said with a nod.

But then she remembered the grim expression on Mike's face and how pale he had looked back by the house. She began to wonder if there were other reasons he had wanted to avoid Mr. Harrington.

"Say, you are going to tell Mr. Harrington about Pretty Lady, aren't you?" Polly wanted to know. "I mean, you're not losing your nerve or your faith in Pretty Lady, are you?"

Mike shook his head and sighed. "No, Polly, I believe in Pretty Lady more than anything in the world," he said. "I promise I'll talk to Mr. Harrington as soon as I feel I can."

Polly saw a small truck driving up to the stable. "That's Joe," Mike told her. "I told him you needed a ride home. He's already put your bike in the truck." Without another word, he turned and went into Pretty Lady's stall.

Polly glanced into the stall and noticed a troubled look in Mike's brown eyes as he began to give Pretty Lady her rubdown. Something is bothering Mike, she thought as she stepped into the truck. I wish I knew what it was.

The next afternoon, when Polly arrived at the front gate of the Harringtons' estate, she rang the stable bell as usual. She waited for a while, and when Mike did not appear, she wheeled her bicycle around to the back of the estate and stepped through the archway, as she had done the first day she had come to visit Pretty Lady.

When she reached the field, she saw the filly grazing. But there was no sign of Mike anywhere.

"Do you know where Mike is?" she asked Joe, who was passing by.

"No, I don't, Miss," Joe replied. "Haven't seen him all day." He gave her a friendly nod and headed toward the stable.

When Pretty Lady saw Polly coming toward her, she nickered softly. "How are you today, girl?" Polly asked as she approached the filly.

As she stroked Pretty Lady, she wondered what had happened to Mike. He hadn't been acting like his usual cheerful self. She thought about how well she and Mike worked together as a team. She also realized what a good friend he had become.

Just then, she spotted a tall, well-dressed man walking toward the field. With him was a bald, heavyset man in a rumpled suit and a boater hat.

The men went over and stood before Polly. "My name is James Harrington," the tall man said in a brisk, businesslike tone. "Who are you and what are you doing here?"

Polly looked up at Mr. Harrington. "I'm Polly Canfield, a friend of Mike, the stable boy."

Mr. Harrington shook his head. "I don't know to whom you're referring," he said curtly. "No one by that name works for me."

As Polly blinked at him in disbelief, he took the reins from her hands and said in the same curt tone, "This horse is a valuable piece of property, young lady. She is not a pet. Now, run along home, like a good girl."

Polly took a few steps back, her face burning with embarrassment.

Mr. Harrington turned to the heavyset man. "You can look her over now, Mr. Baker," he said.

Polly watched as Mr. Baker stepped up to Pretty Lady and examined her teeth. Then he expertly ran his hand along her body and down her legs.

He turned to Mr. Harrington. "She'll do," he said.

"Here's what I'm willing to pay." He named a price.

"That seems fair," Mr. Harrington said, nodding. "But I'll have to think about it. I may be receiving other offers."

Polly stared in horror as she realized what was happening. Mr. Harrington was planning to sell Pretty Lady! She looked at the filly and tears filled her eyes. Then Polly turned and ran.

Polly Takes Charge

P olly, her head down, ran as fast as she could. She didn't know where she was going, and she didn't care. All of sudden, she bumped headfirst into someone. She looked up and saw Mike.

"What is it, Polly?" he asked anxiously. "What's wrong?"

Polly stared at him for a few seconds. Then she demanded angrily, "Who are you, Mike?"

When Mike didn't reply, Polly said hotly, "I just met Mr. Harrington, so I know you're not his stable boy. I want to know who you really are and why you've been lying to me."

Mike looked away from Polly.

"Your name probably isn't even Mike!" Polly added disgustedly.

He turned back to her and said quietly, "My name *is* Mike, Polly. It's short for Michael. Michael Harrington."

Polly clenched her fists in anger. "You're lying again!" she cried. "Michael Harrington is in New York City. He's working as a copyboy on his father's newspaper."

"No, Polly," Mike said, shaking his head. "I was supposed to work there after school got out, but I came to Saratoga instead. See, my father wants me to learn about newspapers, so that I can work in the family business some day. That's *his* dream. I came here to start pursuing *my* dream—to be a professional horse trainer."

Mike hesitated for a moment. Then he said in a desperate tone, "I thought if I could prove to Dad that I could train a winning horse, he'd let me choose my own career. But all that doesn't matter now," he added bitterly. "When Dad found out I wasn't working at the newspaper, he ordered me to go to New York City."

Polly saw the anguished look on Mike's face, and deep down she couldn't help feeling sorry for him. But she was too angry to admit it. "You should have told me the truth instead of lying to me," she said. "I thought we were friends. Didn't you trust me?"

"I never told you I was a stable boy," Mike reminded her. "You assumed I was."

"That doesn't matter," Polly said stubbornly. "You still should have told me who you really were."

"I *was* going to tell you," Mike insisted desperately. "But the more we worked together with Pretty Lady, the harder it became. See, I really liked the way you treated me—like I was a regular guy instead of some spoiled rich kid. That's what you said about the Harringtons' kid the day we began to train Pretty Lady, remember? I was afraid that if I told you I was Mr. Harrington's son, you wouldn't want to be my friend."

"If you think that, then you're hopeless!" Polly told him. "I like you because you're *Mike*. I don't care if you're a stable boy or a rich kid. Just like I love Pretty Lady for herself, not just because she might win an important race."

"You're right," Mike admitted. "I see that now. I'm sorry for not being honest with you, Polly. If I could make it up to you somehow, I would. But it's too late for that. I have to leave for New York tomorrow morning."

Without another word, he turned and walked toward the house.

Polly had never felt so miserable in her whole life. Mike was leaving, and Pretty Lady was never going to get the chance to race. Polly might never see either one of them again.

Before she left forever, Polly wanted to see Pretty Lady one last time. She walked back to the field and, stepping up to the filly, buried her face in her mane. Pretty Lady nickered softly. Then she turned her head and nuzzled Polly's shoulder. Despite her unhappiness, Polly couldn't help noticing that it was the first time Pretty Lady had done that. Somehow, the filly's friendly nuzzle made Polly feel worse than ever.

"Oh, Pretty Lady," she whispered. "I just lost a good friend, and now I'm going to lose you, too. I don't want either you or Mike to go away, but what can I do to stop it?"

As Polly stood there, she began to think hard about what to do next. After several moments, she made up her mind. She gave the filly a last, loving pat, turned, and strode over to the house. She stepped up to the front door, a determined expression on her face, and rapped the brass knocker several times.

The door opened, and a man in a butler's uniform appeared before her. "Yes?" the butler said stiffly.

"I would like to see Mr. Harrington, please," Polly told him, adding quickly, "I'm a friend of his son, Mike."

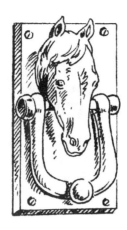

The butler nodded and closed the door. Polly bit her lip and waited for his return. A few moments later, he reappeared. "Mr. Harrington will see you," he said.

Polly followed the butler across the tiled entrance hall, past a long staircase with wide steps and highly polished oak banisters. The butler stopped at a door, opened it, and ushered Polly into a wood-paneled library. Then he closed the door silently behind her, leaving Polly alone with Mike's father.

Mr. Harrington sat behind an oak desk, studying a page from his newspaper. Polly stepped toward the desk and stood before him.

Mr. Harrington put down the newspaper and looked at Polly. Before he could ask her what she wanted, she said boldly, "Mr. Harrington, I don't think you're being fair to Mike or to Pretty Lady. Both of

them deserve a chance to prove themselves. I think you should give them that chance."

Mike's father raised his eyebrows in surprise, but he didn't say anything.

Polly took a deep breath and continued. "Mike and I have been training Pretty Lady for weeks," she said. "She's a different horse now. I know she can win the Travers Stakes." Polly stared into Mr. Harrington's stern eyes. "Mike has worked so hard. Please let him show you what a swell job he's done."

After Polly had finished speaking, Mr. Harrington remained silent. Polly waited anxiously for his reply. After several moments, he nodded gravely at her. "Thank you for being so honest with me, young lady," he said.

He stood up from his desk, turned, and pulled a satin bell rope attached to the wall behind him. A moment later, the door to the library opened, and the Harringtons' butler stepped into the room.

"Hobson, would you show Miss Canfield out, please?" Mr. Harrington said.

"Very good, Sir," the butler replied, holding the door open for Polly.

Polly stared at Mr. Harrington. He picked up the newspaper and began studying it again. "But, Mr. Harrington, you haven't told me what— " she began.

"Thank you, Miss Canfield," he said, looking up briefly. Then he went back to his reading.

Polly turned and slowly left the room. "This way, Miss," the butler said as he led her across the tiled entrance hall to the front door.

Polly walked out of the house, feeling worse than before. She had let Mike and Pretty Lady down, and now she was going to lose the two of them forever.

TWELVE

Mr. Harrington Decides

The next morning, Polly tried to keep herself busy by helping her father with the horses. But all she could think about were Mike and Pretty Lady, and how she would never see them again.

Because it was a hot, sticky day, Polly went back to the house for a glass of lemonade after she had finished her chores. She had just stepped into the front hall, when the phone rang.

It was Hobson, the Harringtons' butler, asking her to call on Mr. Harrington at her earliest convenience.

Polly didn't reply for a moment or two. She felt completely baffled by Mr. Harrington's request.

"May I tell Mr. Harrington that you will call, Miss

Canfield?" the butler asked politely.

"I'll come over right away," Polly said.

Why does Mike's father want to see me? she wondered as she pedaled toward the Harringtons' estate. Maybe Pretty Lady is sick or injured, she thought anxiously. She thought of other possibilities, but none of them made sense. When she reached Mike's house, she was just as puzzled as she had been earlier.

She got off her bicycle, stepped toward the front gate, and pressed the top bell. A few moments later, she saw Hobson, the butler, walking toward her from the house. "Good morning, Miss," he said as he opened the gate. "Mr. Harrington is waiting for you in the library."

Polly followed the butler into the house and back to the library. When she stepped into the room, she was surprised to see that Mike stood in front of his father's desk. Mr. Harrington sat behind the desk, studying some papers in a folder. Polly walked across the room, stood next to Mike, and gave him a questioning look. Mike shrugged, as if to say, "I don't know any more about this than you do."

Mr. Harrington closed the folder and looked first at Polly and then at Mike. "Yesterday, Miss Canfield told me that you have both spent a great deal of time training Pretty Lady to race again," he said to his son in his usual brisk manner. "Is this true?"

"Yes, Father," Mike said. "I wanted to prove to you— "

Mr. Harrington held up his hand. "Let's stick with the subject of Pretty Lady for now," he said quietly.

He turned to Polly. "Last night, I thought about what you said to me, young lady," he told her. "I would like to know if you truly believe Pretty Lady has a chance of winning a race like the Travers Stakes."

Polly felt a glimmer of hope at Mr. Harrington's words. "We really do think she can win, Mr. Harrington," she said eagerly.

She and Mike took turns explaining to him how they had trained the filly on the lunge and how fast she was when they rode her.

"Pretty Lady can still be skittish now and then," Polly said, finally. She told Mr. Harrington what had happened two nights earlier, when the party guests had pestered the filly.

"But that could have happened to just about any high-strung Thoroughbred," Mike was quick to point out, after Polly had finished. "Honestly, Pretty Lady isn't sour toward humans anymore. She obeys and trusts people who treat her right. You should see how high-spirited she is and how fast she can run!"

Mr. Harrington nodded. "I intend to do just that," he said. "I plan to give Pretty Lady a workout on the track. If the filly runs as fast as you and Polly say she does, I'll consider entering her in the Stakes."

Polly and Mike looked at each other joyfully. "Gee, that's swell, Mr. Harrington," Polly said, her eyes shining. "Thank you!"

At the Track

A few mornings later, Polly sat in the back seat of the Harringtons' Cadillac with Mike and his father, as the Harringtons' chauffeur drove them to the racetrack for Pretty Lady's workout. Ahead of them Joe drove the filly in the family's horse truck.

Polly was eager to get to the racetrack to see Pretty Lady work out, but at the same time, she was excited to be riding in a chauffeured motorcar.

"I feel as if I were rich, too, riding in this fancy car," Polly said to Mike with a happy sigh as she settled back comfortably against the upholstered seat.

When Mike didn't reply, Polly saw that he was nervously fingering the stopwatch in his hands.

"Don't worry," she whispered. "Pretty Lady will run at top speed today. I know she will!"

Mike nodded and smiled, but he continued to turn the stopwatch over and over in his hands.

A few moments later, they drove up to the fence that surrounded the oval-shaped racetrack. Polly looked out the window and saw that they were near the grandstand. If everything goes the way we planned, she thought, in two weeks we'll be sitting up there cheering for Pretty Lady in the Travers Stakes.

The chauffeur got out of the car and opened the door on Polly's side. Polly stepped out, followed by Mike and his father.

Mr. Harrington led the way to the truck, where Joe guided Pretty Lady down the back ramp. Polly saw the filly shake her head up and down several times, · but she willingly followed Joe's lead.

"She's in high spirits this morning, Sir," Joe said to Mr. Harrington as he saddled her. "But she's given me no trouble so far."

Just then, a short, slim man in a polo shirt, knickers, riding boots, and a cap walk toward them. The man stepped up to Mike's father and took off his cap. "Well, Mr. Harrington, I'm here, just as you asked," he said with a smile. "Now, where's this filly you want me to ride?"

"Thank you for coming on such short notice, Danny," Mr. Harrington said. Then he turned to Polly and Mike. "This is Danny Peterson," he told them. "One of the finest jockeys around. I've hired him to be my personal jockey. Pretty Lady will be the first horse he races for me. If," he added, "I decide to enter her in the Travers."

He led Danny over to Pretty Lady. Polly and Mike followed behind. Danny mounted Pretty Lady and guided her through an opening in the fence onto the track. He warmed her up by taking her on a slow circuit around the track. Then he urged her into a gallop. Mike pressed the button on the stopwatch and timed them, as Danny and Pretty Lady breezed along the track. After Danny had ridden her for a quarter of a mile, Mike checked the stopwatch.

"Well?" Mr. Harrington said, turning to his son.

Mike smiled broadly at his father. "Twenty-three seconds," he said proudly. "And Danny wasn't even riding her at blazing speed, the way he would in the race."

99

"And Pretty Lady's time is even faster than Challenger's," Polly said with delight. "I knew she could do it!"

Mr. Harrington looked pleased as he waved at Danny to keep going. The jockey and Pretty Lady continued to breeze down the track in quarter-mile sections. Mike clocked her speed at each quarter mile. When the jockey had finished the full mile-and-a-quarter circuit that marked the length of the Travers Stakes race, he slowed the filly down and rode her over to Polly, Mike, and Mr. Harrington.

"This filly of yours is a real pleasure to ride," Danny said. "She sure shows speed, and she's responsive. How come you've been keeping her under wraps all year?"

Mr. Harrington smiled at Polly and Mike. "I've made up my mind. I'm entering Pretty Lady in the Travers Stakes."

Polly and Mike looked at each other, their faces lit up with joy. "That's swell, Mr, Harrington," Polly said. "I just knew you'd change your mind about Pretty Lady once you saw her on the track."

"Well, young lady," Mike's father said with a twinkle in his eye. "It looks as if you were right."

"And They're Off!"

Every morning after that, Polly and Mike went over to the track to watch Danny exercise Pretty Lady. Their training of Pretty Lady was over, but they enjoyed seeing her improve under Danny's care.

A few days before the race, Polly and Mike sat in the Harringtons' stable office, looking at the local newspaper. They studied the paper each day to see which horses were running in the Travers Stakes and which horses had dropped out. Polly knew from her father that Mr. Sinclair had entered Challenger.

"Look," Mike said suddenly. "This article about the Travers says that more owners have pulled their horses out of the race."

Polly took the newspaper from him and read out loud, "Many in Saratoga's racing world believe it is the presence of a speedy Thoroughbred named Challenger, and that steady prizewinner, Lucky Star, that has convinced the rest of the owners to withdraw their horses from the Travers. Now the only entries are Challenger, Lucky Star, and a long shot named Pretty Lady, owned by Mr. James Harrington. This reporter wonders: Will Mr. Harrington pull his filly out of the race, too?"

Polly put the paper down. "Of course, Pretty Lady is going to stay in the race," she said indignantly. Then she looked at Mike, her eyes wide. "This means that the Travers Stakes will be only a three-horse race, Mike!"

"I know," Mike said with a worried expression. "It's exciting, but it also means that everyone will be watching Pretty Lady to see how she competes against the two fastest horses in Saratoga."

"Pretty Lady is faster than Challenger, and I bet she can beat Lucky Star, too," Polly said confidently. "Trust me."

"I do," Mike said. "And I trust Pretty Lady, too. I know that she'll run on Saturday like she's never run before."

When the afternoon of the Travers Stakes finally

arrived, Polly felt almost as skittish as Pretty Lady had once been as she drove over to the racetrack with her parents. Sam, the Canfields' groom, had left in the horse truck with Challenger earlier.

"Stop fidgeting so much," Laura Canfield told her daughter gently. "We'll be there soon."

"Polly can't help it, dear," Bill Canfield said to his wife with a chuckle. "After all, it's not every day our daughter has the chance to race a horse against one that has been trained by her own father."

"Will you be angry if Pretty Lady wins instead of Challenger, Dad?" Polly asked.

"I'll be disappointed," Bill Canfield admitted. "But I'll be very proud of you. Your happiness is more important to me than whether or not Challenger wins today."

"Thanks for being such a good sport, Dad," Polly said, adding with a grin, "especially since you know that Pretty Lady is going to win the race."

Her father laughed. "Well, we'll see about that," he said good-naturedly. "You never know what can happen in a horse race!"

A few moments later, Bill Canfield pulled into the racetrack parking area. Polly and her parents got out of the car and walked over to the paddock, the closed-in area where the horses were saddled.

"And They're Off!"

As Polly approached the paddock, she glanced at the grandstand and saw that it was crowded with people. Another crowd of spectators lined the fence that surrounded the racetrack. Still more spectators filled the grassy, fenced-in oval inside the track. There were three high poles in the grassy area, with signs attached to them. The signs displayed the names of the jockeys and the horses they were riding today. Polly knew that, after the race, another sign would announce the names of the winning horse and jockey. When Polly and her parents reached the paddock, Polly saw Mr. Harrington, Mike, and Danny Peterson standing by Pretty Lady. The jockey looked wonderful in his blue-and-white silk racing uniform.

Polly introduced her parents to Mike and his father. Then Bill Canfield said, "I'm afraid you'll have to excuse me, Mr. Harrington. I need to speak to Challenger's owner and to his jockey."

"I understand," Mr. Harrington said graciously. "Good luck to you, Mr. Canfield."

"The same to you, Sir," Polly's father said. He smiled at his daughter and gave her a wink. Then he walked off toward Challenger.

"It's a quarter to three," Mike said, glancing at his watch. "Fifteen minutes until post time."

Danny Peterson nodded, swung himself onto

Pretty Lady's back, and placed his feet into the short stirrups of the racing saddle. The filly began to prance back and forth, but Polly could tell from the forward position of her ears and the rippling muscles of her body that she was feeling high-spirited rather than nervous.

"She's ready to go," Danny said, echoing Polly's thoughts.

She and Mike stepped up to Pretty Lady. "Fly like the wind, girl," Mike said, giving the filly a pat.

Polly put her arms around Pretty Lady and kissed her silky neck. "Good luck, girl," she whispered. "We'll be cheering for you."

Just then, they heard the bugle call that told the horses and their jockeys it was time to parade to the starting line. Polly and Mike stepped back and watched with pride as Pretty Lady joined Challenger and Lucky Star in the parade from the paddock to the starting line. As the three horses approached the barriers that marked the start of the race, Polly and Mike could hear wild cheers and loud applause coming from the grandstand.

"We'd better find our seats, quick," Polly said to Mike. "The race will begin any minute!"

The two of them hurried out of the paddock and toward the grandstand. "There's my father and your parents," Mike said, pointing to a row in the grandstand that was right in front of the starting line. They rushed up the steps and found two empty seats next to Mike's father.

Polly turned to face the track and saw that the three horses were lined up behind the starting post, with Pretty Lady in the center. A hush came over the crowd. Polly crossed her fingers and waited.

A moment later, the starter dropped the flag. The horses sprinted forward, and at the same time, the crowd in the grandstand yelled, "And they're off!"

The race was on!

CHAPTER
FIFTEEN

The Race

Polly and Mike watched breathlessly as Challenger, Pretty Lady, and Lucky Star pounded along the track neck and neck. The filly gained speed and edged past Lucky Star at the turn. Rounding the bend, she broke free from the two horses.

"Go, Pretty Lady, go!" Polly yelled.

Pretty Lady stayed in front down the length of the straightaway. Then Challenger started to pick up speed, and Pretty Lady began to fall behind him. Seconds later, Lucky Star gained on both of them. But Pretty Lady, urged on by Danny, broke free again, passed both horses around the next bend, and breezed down the straightaway. Polly and Mike cheered wildly for her, almost as if they hoped that she could hear them.

Pretty Lady fell back, surged ahead, fell back, and gained again.

Then it happened. At the last turn before the final approach to the finish line, Pretty Lady stumbled.

The crowd gasped in unison.

Challenger and Lucky Star sped by Pretty Lady. To Polly and Mike's relief, Danny quickly steadied her. He urged the filly back to top speed, and soon she was edging past Lucky Star. But as she approached the finish line, she was almost a full length behind Challenger.

"I can't watch," Polly said with a groan. She covered her eyes with her hands and waited for the race to be over.

"Look, Polly, look!" she heard Mike yell suddenly. "I can't believe what's happening!"

Polly took her hands away from her eyes just in time to see Pretty Lady sprint forward. The crowd rose to its feet as she went neck and neck with Challenger and then passed him. With a good foot to spare between her and the colt, Pretty Lady dashed across the finish line first.

The crowd roared with excitement. "She did it!" Polly cried as she and Mike hugged each other. "I

knew she could win, and she did!"

Mike grinned at her and then turned to shake hands with his father. "Come on," Mike said, after Polly had hugged her parents. "Let's get down to the winner's circle."

Polly and Mike hurried out of the grandstand, followed by Polly's parents and Mr. Harrington. They reached the enclosure near the track where the awards were given at the same time as a crowd of newspaper reporters and photographers.

A moment later, Danny rode into the winner's circle and brought Pretty Lady to a halt. The Canfields and the Harringtons rushed toward them.

Polly stroked Pretty Lady. "You won, girl!" she said excitedly. "I'm so proud of you!"

"Congratulations, Danny," Mr. Harrington said, shaking the jockey's hand. "You did a fine job out there today. But then, you had a fine horse to ride."

"I'd say so," Danny replied, reaching over to pat Pretty Lady.

Just then, an official of the racetrack approached them, holding a wreath of flowers. Polly watched, her eyes shining with joy, as the official placed the horseshoe-shaped wreath around Pretty Lady's neck.

The official cleared his throat. "And now," he said, "I would like to award this check and trophy to you,

Mr. Harrington, as the owner of this year's Travers Stakes winner, Pretty Lady."

Polly felt as though she would burst with pride.

"What do you plan to do with the money, Mr. Harrington?" one of the reporters asked.

"I'm donating it to Pretty Lady's trainers, Polly Canfield and my son, Mike," he replied. "Without their faith in Pretty Lady, we wouldn't be standing in the winner's circle today."

Polly felt pleased and proud. She looked at Mike. From the way he was smiling, she was sure he felt the same way.

After the reporters and photographers had left the enclosure, Danny climbed off Pretty Lady's back and carefully removed the wreath from her neck. The filly snorted and tossed her head in a spirited manner.

"She wants to have another breeze around that track," Mike said with a laugh.

Mr. Harrington turned to his son and smiled. "She'll have that chance again soon," he said. "But she wouldn't have had any chance at all, if you hadn't believed in her or in yourself. You've proved to me that you have the makings of a fine horse trainer, just like your grandfather. If that's the career you want, son, I won't stand in your way."

"Thank you, Father," Mike said.

Then Mr. Harrington turned to Polly, his eyes twinkling. "I have you to thank, young lady, for helping me understand about Mike and Pretty Lady," he said. "I want you to know that I've decided not to sell Pretty Lady, and I hope that you'll feel free to visit her as often as you'd like."

"Thank you, Mr. Harrington," Polly said, smiling back at him.

That night, there was a victory party for Pretty Lady at the Harringtons' mansion. Polly felt a twinge of excitement as she stepped onto the patio behind the house with her parents. She felt grown up and stylish in her pretty new dress, and she was glad that she had let her mother curl her short hair with a curling iron.

Polly gazed at the glittering scene around her. "Everything looks exactly like it did that other night," she said to Mike when he came up to her. "Only this time, I'm not just watching the party. I'm a guest!"

Suddenly, she noticed that Mike's hair was slicked back and that he was wearing a tuxedo. She had never seen him so dressed up before. "You look nice," she said. "You don't look the way you usually do, like—"

"Like a stable boy?" Mike asked with a grin.

"Right!" Polly said, laughing.

113

Just then, the band struck up a Charleston. "Come on," Polly said eagerly, grabbing Mike's hand. "Let's dance!"

Together they headed for the center of the patio and began to dance to the music. They grinned at each other as they crossed their hands over their knees in the style of the popular dance.

"That was fun," Polly said, when the dance was over. She and Mike walked toward the big fountain. Polly looked at the beautiful mansion silhouetted against the moonlight and the stylishly dressed guests laughing, talking, and dancing. She sighed happily and thought that she had never been to such a wonderful party before in her whole life.

But she couldn't forget who had helped to make all this possible. She excused herself and began to walk away.

"Where are you going?" Mike asked in surprise.

"I have to see someone," Polly said to him over her shoulder as she hurried away. "I'll be right back!"

She ran across the lawn, through the hedge, and to the stable.

Pretty Lady was looking out the top door of her stall. When she sensed Polly's presence, she nickered softly. Polly stepped up to her and stroked her neck gently. "You won the Travers Stakes today, girl!" she

114

said softly to the filly. "I knew all the time that you could do it."

Pretty Lady tossed her head and whinnied as if to say that *she* had known all along that she could do it, too.

FACTS
ABOUT THE BREED

You probably know a lot about Thoroughbreds from reading this book. Here are some more interesting facts about this swift-footed breed.

∩ Thoroughbreds generally stand between 15.3 and 16.2 hands. Instead of using feet and inches, all horses are measured in hands and inches. A hand is equal to four inches.

∩ Thoroughbreds are usually brown, bay (brown with black mane, tail, and lower leg), chestnut (reddish brown all over), black, or gray.

∩ Thoroughbreds, like Arabians, have thin skin. Often the veins in the head are visible beneath the skin.

Ω Thoroughbreds are the fastest horses in the world. Some can run faster than 50 miles an hour.

Ω While Thoroughbreds have great courage, stamina, and athletic ability, they can be nervous, high strung, and temperamental.

Ω All Thoroughbred horses that race receive their very own registration number. When the horse is two years old, this number is tattooed on the inside of its upper lip so that the horse can always be positively identified.

Ω The first digit of the registration number is actually a letter. Every horse born in the same year gets a registration number that starts with the same letter. For example, horses born in 1992 have registration numbers starting with a V. Those born in 1993 got numbers starting with W and so on through the alphabet. If you were a Thoroughbred, what letter would your registration number start with?

∩ The Thoroughbred was first developed in England in the seventeenth and eighteenth centuries. Three Arabian horses are regarded as the founding sires, or fathers, of the Thoroughbred breed—the Byerly Turk, the Darley Arabian, and the Godolphin Arabian. These three stallions were bred to the native race horses to produce the Thoroughbred.

∩ Thoroughbreds are popular all over the world. There are major Thoroughbred racing and breeding centers in England, Ireland, the United States, and France. Excellent Thoroughbreds are also raised in Australia, New Zealand, and Italy.

∩ Horse racing has been popular in England for hundreds of years. After regaining the throne in 1660, Charles II did much to promote racing, known as the sport of kings. Charles II encouraged the common people to attend races and even rode in them himself.

∩ The most famous Thoroughbred race in the United States is the Kentucky Derby. Run every year in the beginning of May since 1875, the 1 $\frac{1}{4}$-mile long Derby is a race for three-year-olds.

∩ Three races—the Kentucky Derby, the Preakness Stakes, and the Belmont Stakes—make up the Triple Crown, racing's most glamorous prize.

∩ Only eleven horses have won the Triple Crown—Sir Barton in 1919, Gallant Fox in 1930, Omaha in 1935, War Admiral in 1937, Whirlaway in 1941, Count Fleet in 1943, Assault in 1946, Citation in 1948, Secretariat in 1973, Seattle Slew in 1977, and Affirmed in 1978.

∩ Man O'War was one of the most famous Thoroughbred race horses ever. Also known as "Big Red," he was beaten in a race only once and that was when he was just two years old. He died in 1947, and more than one thousand people went to his funeral. He is buried in the Kentucky Horse Park near Lexington, Kentucky, where a statue in his likeness stands proudly as a tribute to the horse.

∩ Citation was another very famous Thoroughbred. Foaled in 1945, Citation was the first race horse to win a million dollars. Citation was so fast that when he ran the Preakness Stakes as a three year old, he ran alone. No other horse dared to challenge him!

∩ Secretariat, the Triple Crown winner in 1973, still holds the speed record for both the Kentucky Derby and the Belmont Stakes.

∩ Thoroughbreds have played an important role in the development of other breeds of horses. In 1756, Janus, a chestnut Thoroughbred stallion, was brought to Virginia from England. Janus, a grandson of the Godolphin Arabian, was bred to the local racing mares and became one of the foundation sires of the American Quarter Horse.

∩ Besides serving as race horses, Thoroughbreds also excel as hunters, polo ponies, steeplechasers, and in the dressage ring.